1

OUR FRIEND
MIKEY THE LIZARD

MIkey The LIZARD

LIVES IN A TREE

HE IS A GREEN LIZARD

AS GREEN AS COULD BE

4

HE CRAWLS ALONG BRANCHES

THE MANGOES TO SEE

MIKEY THE LIZARD

IS SMILING AT ME

MIKEY, MIKEY WE CALL OUT TO HIM!

MIKEY THE LZARD NOW HANGS ON A LIMB

COME ON DOWN MIKEY

SO FRIENDS WE CAN BE

DON'T BE AFRAD MIKEY

We ARE FRIENDS YOU'll SEE

LIZARDS ARE FRIENDLY

AND AS NICE AS COULD BE

LIKE OUR LIZARD FRIEND MIKEY

WHO LIVES IN THE MANGO TREE

SLOWLY HE WALKS

HIS EYES OPEN WIDE

12

MIKEY THE LIZARD

EATS SPIDERS AND FLIES

13

ON VEGETABLES AND FRUITS
HE ALSO RELIES

SOME OF MIKEY'S Family & Friends

ARE NOT GREEN BUT ARE BROWN

SOME LIVE ON TREES

AND SOME ON THE GROUND

SOME LIZARDS ARE BIG

AND SOME ARE SMALL

18

SOME LIZARDS ARE SHORT

AND SOME ARE TALL

AND THOUGH THEY ARE DIFFERENT

MIKEY LOVES THEM ALL

MIKEY OUR FRIEND THE LIZARD

IS AS NICE AS CAN BE

23

HE RESPECTS ALL THE LIZARDS
IN HIS COMMUNITY

LIKE LIZARDS

PEOPLE ARE DIFFERENT TOO

27

Sources and Acknowledgements

The images used for this book are taken directly from free and royalty

free stock images and photo sources available online.

https://www.google.com/search?q=many+lizards+together&tbm=isch&ved=2ahUKEwiL8bGgkfbuAhUCOt8KHbhWAJoQ2-cCegQ

https://www.google.com/search?q=free+images+and+royalty+free+stock&tbm=isch&ved=2ahUKEwj56dbkv_buAhURA98KHfeSB

https://htmlcolorcodes.com/resources/ultimate-guide-to-free-stock-photos/

https://www.istockphoto.com/photos/free

https://www.pexels.com/